Sportsercise!

A "School" Story About Exercise-Induced Asthma

by
Kim Gosselin

Published by
JayJo Books, LLC.

<u>SPORTSercise!</u>
A "School" Story About Exercise-Induced Asthma
Copyright © 1997, by Kim Gosselin.
First Edition. All rights reserved. No part of this book may be reproduced in any manner whatsoever without written permission from the publisher. For information address: JayJo Books, LLC., P.O. Box 213, Valley Park, MO 63088-0213. Printed in the United States of America.

Published by
JayJo Books, LLC.
P.O. Box 213
Valley Park, MO 63088-0213

Edited by Barbara A. Mitchell

Library of Congress Cataloging-in-Publication Data
Gosselin, Kim
SPORTSercise!/Kim Gosselin – First Edition
Library of Congress Catalog Card Number 97-71951

Searching Notes:
Children's Literature

ISBN 0-9639449-8-3
Library of Congress

Proud publishers of the *Special Kids in School*® series written to educate peers of children living with chronic conditions and/or special needs.

IF YOU HAVE ASTHMA, JOIN OUR CLUB!

**Call
1-800-982-3902
and Join Today!**

A UNIQUE CLUB
FOR CHILDREN WITH ASTHMA

Asthma Explorers is an educational program sponsored by, and is a registered service mark of, Rhône-Poulenc Rorer Pharmaceuticals Inc.

The publication of **SPORTSercise!** was made possible through a generous Educational Grant by Rhône-Poulenc Rorer Pharmaceuticals Inc.

Acknowledgements

A special thanks to Kristin, Terrie and Susan
of the American Lung Association, St. Louis, Missouri,
who provide me with continuous support and encouragement.

A portion of the sale of this book is donated specifically to help fund medical research and education. Thank you for your support.

All books published by JayJo Books, LLC. are available at special quantity discounts when purchased in bulk by corporations, organizations, or groups. Special imprints, messages, logos and excerpts can be produced to meet your needs. For more information, call (800) 801-0159.

*The opinions expressed in **<u>SPORTSercise!</u>** are those solely of the author. Allergy and asthma care are highly individualized. One should **never** alter allergy or asthma care without first consulting a member of the individual's professional medical team.

*Dedicated to my favorite basketball player,
Jayson, whose courage and zest for the
game of life inspire me every day.*

The sounds of rustling paper and children's chatter greeted Mr. Flemming as he glided into his morning classroom. In just a couple of days the school's annual sports festival, dubbed "SPORTSercise," would begin. Mr. Flemming's class would be taking part in the three-legged relay, the potato sack race, and the "hoops" competition!

Mr. Flemming slid his notes under the bright red football helmet sitting upside down atop his desk. Torn slips of notebook paper spilled over the sides. On each one a single name had been carefully scrawled in pencil.

"Okay," shouted Mr. Flemming, bringing the classroom to attention. "We're ready to draw names for our class teams. Justin, would you and Ashley help me out? And, while you're here, I found something that belongs to you."

Justin looked up and saw his asthma relief inhaler resting on Mr. Flemming's desk. "Thanks, Mr. Flemming. I guess I forgot to put it away," he added in dismay.

The day before, Justin had used his asthma relief inhaler right after recess. While he was playing soccer, his chest started hurting and feeling tight. Soon he was coughing a lot too! Lately, Justin's asthma had been acting up every time he played sports or exercised.

Mr. Flemming thought Justin would be happy to help choose names for the "SPORTSercise" teams. He shuffled up to the front of the room and picked up his inhaler. "He sure doesn't look very happy," thought Mr. Flemming.

Justin's friend Ashley (who had asthma, too) looked thrilled to have been selected! She smiled from ear to ear as she announced the first name drawn.

"Michael!" she exclaimed, with excitement.

Children's cheers echoed in the classroom as Michael went up to print his name on the board. Justin dug in and scooped out another scrawled piece of paper.

"Emily," he whispered, his head hanging down.

"Speak up, we can't hear you," said Mr. Flemming. The teacher wondered what was troubling Justin. He decided to speak to him after class.

Soon, all the kids had been picked for teams. Mr. Flemming explained how their class would compete against teams from another teacher's class. It was old Mrs. Hatfield's class!! Mr. Flemming's class had the worst luck. Old Mrs. Hatfield had taken part in over twelve "SPORTSercise" festivals. She'd been at the school FOREVER!!!! Worse yet, her class never lost a competition!

"Okay, class," said Mr. Flemming, as he finished organizing the names on the board. "You all know we're going to have to work extra hard this year. Mrs. Hatfield's class is tough to beat." Glancing at his wristwatch, he added, "Now get off to gym class before you're late," and shooed them out the door.

Justin was about to leave when Mr. Flemming asked if he could speak to him. "What's bothering you, Justin?"

"Um…" Justin said hesitatingly. "I don't want to take part in 'SPORTSercise' this year."

"Why not?" asked Mr. Flemming with disbelief. "You're one of our very best teammates."

"My asthma has been bugging me lately every time I exercise," said Justin. "I'm afraid I'll get sick, or worse yet, wreck things for the whole class," he added in despair.

"Well, we certainly can't have you getting sick," said Mr. Flemming. "Let's take a trip down to see Mrs. Hardy, the school nurse. I bet she's got an answer for us."

Mrs. Hardy greeted Justin's entrance with a warm smile. A younger girl was sitting next to her, using her asthma inhaler.

"Lots of kids living with asthma are sometimes bothered by exercise," she said. Mrs. Hardy went on to remind Justin that exercise was an asthma "trigger," or something that could cause an asthma episode.

"In fact," she said, "that's what happened to this little gal. She started having trouble breathing during gym class."

"She did?" Justin asked, surprised. "You mean I'm not the only one?"

"Of course not! Exercise (like playing sports) is a very common asthma trigger." Mrs. Hardy telephoned Justin's mom. Justin's mother assured Mrs. Hardy that she would let his asthma doctor know, too. That way, Justin's doctor could prescribe the right kind of medicine for him. She soon called back, telling the nurse that Justin's doctor would see him right after school.

"I bet you'll be feeling much better by the time the festival begins," Mrs. Hardy said. "Besides, your class really needs you!"

"Thanks, Mrs. Hardy," Justin said, hugging her tight.

Justin sat on Dr. Casey's examining table while she listened to his lungs. She talked to him about his feelings and some of his asthma symptoms. Next, she asked him to blow big puffs of air into a peak-flow meter. Dr. Casey reminded him that playing sports, like other ways of exercising, could be an asthma trigger. As the school nurse had told him before, lots of kids (just like Justin) lived with exercise-induced asthma.

"There are many different kinds of asthma medicines," Dr. Casey went on to explain. "Some inhalers help control asthma for a long time; some give quick relief (like during an asthma episode); and some do both!"

"Let's try a medication that might be best for you," Dr. Casey told him, with a smile. She handed his mother a new prescription, and asked her to please call back later to tell her how it was working.

The rest of the week flew by, as teachers and students alike prepared for the grand "SPORTSercise" festival.

Justin noticed the school nurse had her own special booth, right in the middle of the festival grounds! He took his turn in line, waiting for his medication. The nurse had been right, Justin thought. Besides Ashley, he saw lots of other kids using inhalers and taking asthma medicine too! For kids who had exercise-induced asthma, it was important to use their asthma medicine BEFORE exercising to prevent asthma episodes from happening!

Justin checked his peak-flow reading and saw that his number was in the green zone (for GOOD control). Justin used his new inhaler and waited (at least ten to twenty minutes) before going off to exercise. That way, his exercise-induced asthma medicine would work its very best. "Be sure to come back and see me if you start having asthma symptoms," Mrs. Hardy told him. Justin grinned and scampered off to take his place in the first competition of the day: the three-legged race!

Ashley was ahead of him and already waiting. He took his place next to her while Mr. Flemming tied their legs together. Seconds later the starting whistle shrieked. Ashley and Justin took off and gave it their best try. They tripped and fell down twice, laughing hysterically. Ashley and Justin's relay team came in second place. A team from old Mrs. Hatfield's class came in first (of course).

Next it was time for the potato sack race. Ashley and Justin each crawled into enormous old flour sacks. Soon they were off, tumbling towards the bright yellow "finish" banner. In spite of their mighty efforts, Ashley and Justin's team came in fourth place.

Feeling a little sad, the two friends decided to take a rest. They grabbed a cool glass of lemonade in the food court and shared a bag of popcorn. Since Ashley was having a little trouble breathing, she ran to the nurse's booth to check her peak-flow reading. Justin felt great! His new asthma medicine really seemed to be working!

A few minutes later, Justin and Ashley caught up with each other at the final competition of the day. The "hoops" event was their very favorite. It was worth triple the points of any other competition. Whoever won the "hoops" event took home the festival trophy!

"I was in the green zone," Ashley called out to Justin, referring to the peak-flow reading she had a few minutes before.

"Great!" yelled back Justin, scoring the first two points of the basketball game.

Soon, the "hoops" event really started heating up. As expected, Mrs. Hatfield's class was leading the competition. This would be the last chance for Mr. Flemming's team to win the golden trophy!

Bleachers of kids rooted and screamed for their favorite teams. Each took turns shooting baskets and scoring points. Mrs. Hatfield's class was in the lead. The clock ticked off. With just a minute to go, Ashley made a basket to tie the game!

Mrs. Hatfield's team had the ball once again. Tension mounted when their tallest kid leapt for a lay-up. He missed!!! Ashley rebounded and dribbled the ball back down the court. Justin waited for the pass.

He knew he only had a matter of seconds to shoot a basket. If he made it, Mr. Flemming's class would win the trophy!!

Just when he jumped to take his shot, the tall kid grabbed his arm! The whistle shrieked. "FOUL!" called the referee!! Justin took his place for a free throw. Now he had two chances to score a point and win the game. Ashley held her breath. Justin took his shot. The basketball hit the outside rim of the hoop. No score. One last chance!

"SWOOSH" went the basketball through the hoop! Justin did it!! Mr. Flemming's class won the game! The crowd went wild, hoisting Justin up and carrying him off the court. A few minutes later, Mr. Flemming presented Justin with the class's treasured trophy.

Justin was overjoyed!! Winning the "SPORTSercise" trophy meant almost everything to him. More importantly, Justin discovered that sometimes, with help from doctors and the right medicine, it was possible to help prevent asthma episodes. As long as his asthma was in good control, Justin could play and win at almost anything. Even sports and exercise!

To order additional copies of **SPORTSercise!** contact your local bookstore or library.
Or call the publisher directly at (314) 861-1331 or (800) 801-0159.

Write to us at:
JayJo Books, LLC.
P.O. Box 213
Valley Park, MO 63088-0213

Ask about our special quantity discounts for schools, hospitals, and affiliated organizations.
Fax us at (314) 861-2411.

Look for other books by Kim Gosselin including:

From our *Special Kids in School*® series:

Taking Diabetes to School

Taking Asthma to School

Taking Seizure Disorders to School

Others:
Taking Asthma to Camp
A Fictional Story About Asthma Camp

ZooAllergy
A Fun Story About Allergy and Asthma Triggers

and new titles coming soon: **Smoking STINKS!!**
From our new *Substance Free Kids* series.

A portion of the proceeds from all our publications is donated to various charities to help fund important medical research and education. We work hard to make a difference in the lives of children with chronic conditions and/or special needs. Thank you for your support.

Kim Gosselin

ABOUT THE AUTHOR

Kim Gosselin was born and raised in Michigan where she attended Central Michigan University. She began her professional writing career shortly after her two young sons were both diagnosed with chronic illnesses. Kim is extremely committed to bringing the young reader quality children's health education while raising important funds for medical research.

Kim now resides and writes in Missouri. She is an avid supporter of the Epilepsy Foundation of America, the American Lung Association, and a member of the American Diabetes Association, the Juvenile Diabetes Foundation International, the Society of Children's Book Writers and Illustrators, the Small Publishers Association of North America, the Publishers Marketing Association, and The Author's Guild.